GRAPHIC SURVIVAL STORIES

DEFYING DEATH IN THE
DESERT

by Gary Jeffrey

illustrated by Emanuele Boccanfuso

First published in UK in 2010 by
Evans Brothers Limited
2A Portman Mansions
Chiltern Street
London
W1U 6NR

First published in the USA in 2010 by
The Rosen Publishing Group, Inc. 29 East 21st Street, New York, 10010

Designed and produced by
David West Children's Books
7 Princeton Court
55 Felsham Road
London SW15 1AZ

Photo credits:
P4 Luca Galuzzi - www.galuzzi.it; p4r, Elmar Thiel; p5t, Chris Brown; p5r, Garrondo;
p5b, kaibara87; p6t, Bernard Gagnon; p6tr, Fritz Geller-Grimm; p6m, Nick Fraser;
p6bl, John O'Neill; p7t, CroTigerhawkvok; p7, 2John Spooner; p44b, elwonger; p45t,
jared; p45b, Ancheta Wis.

British Library Cataloguing-in-Publication Data
A catalogue record for this book is available from the British Library

Printed in China

ISBN 9780237543273

CONTENTS

THE WORLD'S DESERTS

The word *desert* means "an abandoned place" and for good reason — deserts have almost zero rainfall. No water means there is no plant cover, which means there is little food. Deserts are some of the harshest environments on the planet.

SCORCHED EARTH

A desert is any place where water evaporates faster than rain can replenish it. The lack of moist air means there is little cloud cover to screen the sun. Daytime air temperatures can rise to over 50°C (122°F). After sunset the heat quickly disappears, giving chilly nights. Frequent high winds whip up sandstorms that scour the landscape.

"Cold" deserts like the Gobi Desert, and coastal deserts, like the Namib, also exist. The driest place on Earth is the Atacama Desert in Chile.

Great Basin Desert

Mojave Desert

Sonoran Desert

Sechura Desert

Gobi Desert

Atacama Desert

Patagonia Desert

Kalahari Desert

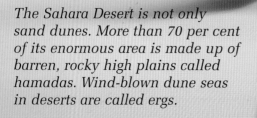

The Sahara Desert is not only sand dunes. More than 70 per cent of its enormous area is made up of barren, rocky high plains called hamadas. Wind-blown dune seas in deserts are called ergs.

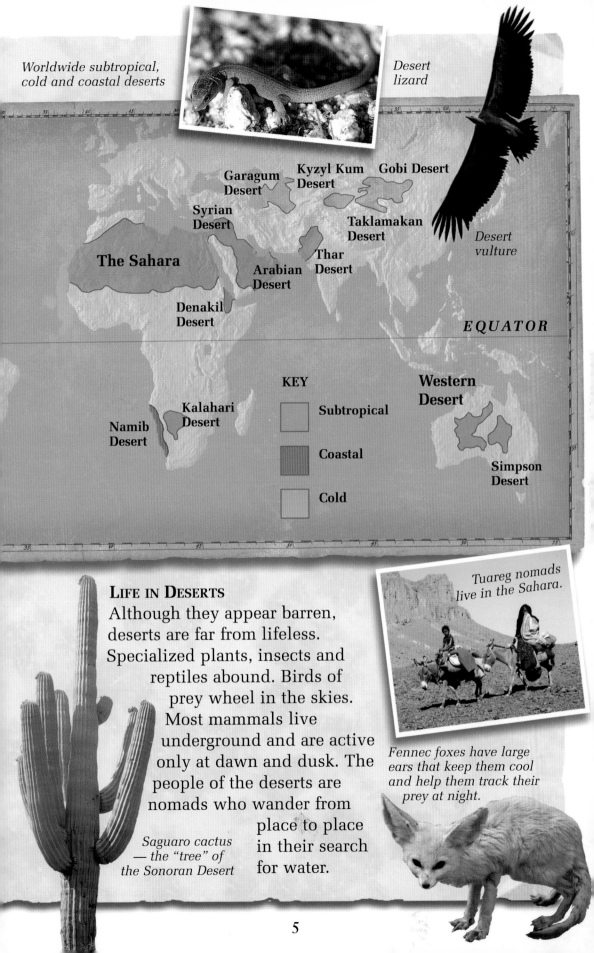

Desert lizard

Garagum Desert

Kyzyl Kum Desert

Gobi Desert

Syrian Desert

Taklamakan Desert

The Sahara

Thar Desert

Arabian Desert

Denakil Desert

Desert vulture

EQUATOR

KEY

Western Desert

Kalahari Desert

Namib Desert

☐ Subtropical

☐ Coastal

☐ Cold

Simpson Desert

LIFE IN DESERTS

Although they appear barren, deserts are far from lifeless. Specialized plants, insects and reptiles abound. Birds of prey wheel in the skies. Most mammals live underground and are active only at dawn and dusk. The people of the deserts are nomads who wander from place to place in their search for water.

Saguaro cactus — the "tree" of the Sonoran Desert

Tuareg nomads live in the Sahara.

Fennec foxes have large ears that keep them cool and help them track their prey at night.

DESERT SURVIVAL

Majestic ergs, towering cliffs, the epic vistas of salt flats — deserts are some of the most awesome places on the planet. Just don't try to live there!

DRY AS DUST

Animals that live in the desert have evolved special ways to save or replace their body fluid. Humans are not so well adapted and in arid conditions will quickly become as dry as mummies if deprived of

Landscapes like Monument Valley, Utah, attract many desert visitors.

water. Intense ultraviolet light can burn even the darkest skin to a crisp if left unprotected. Abrasive winds carrying sand can limit visibility and make life unbearable. Despite this, people can survive in the desert.

A nomad

COPY THE NATIVES

Nomads wear long, loose-fitting clothes that shield them from the worst of the sun and allow air to flow around their skin. They are also masters at making the most of limited resources, whether these are camels, spring-fed oases or edible roots. Nomads sometimes go a long time between meals. They know that water is more important than food.

Camels are used for transportation, milk, clothing, meat and even water.

A Saharan oasis

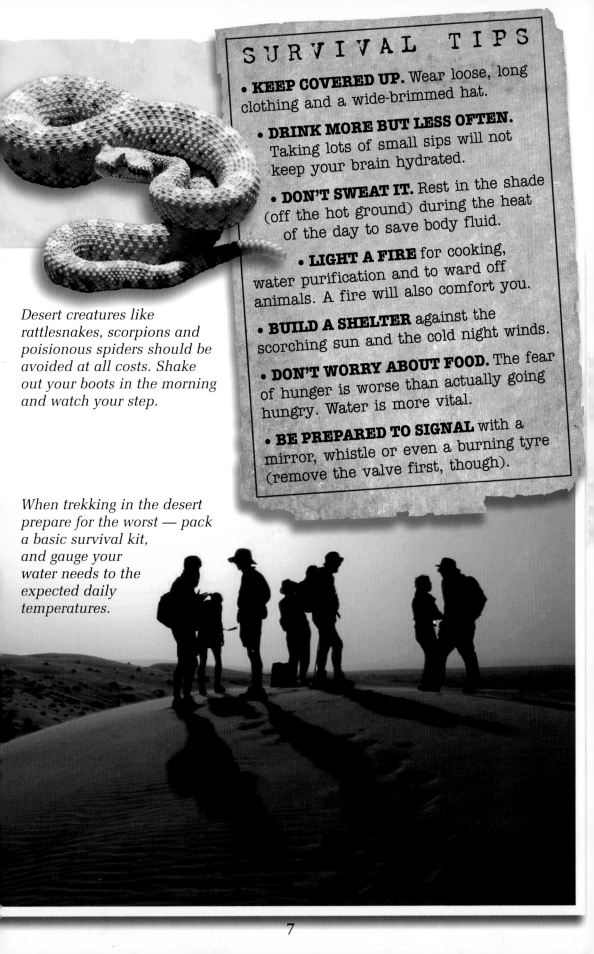

SURVIVAL TIPS

- **KEEP COVERED UP.** Wear loose, long clothing and a wide-brimmed hat.

- **DRINK MORE BUT LESS OFTEN.** Taking lots of small sips will not keep your brain hydrated.

- **DON'T SWEAT IT.** Rest in the shade (off the hot ground) during the heat of the day to save body fluid.

- **LIGHT A FIRE** for cooking, water purification and to ward off animals. A fire will also comfort you.

- **BUILD A SHELTER** against the scorching sun and the cold night winds.

- **DON'T WORRY ABOUT FOOD.** The fear of hunger is worse than actually going hungry. Water is more vital.

- **BE PREPARED TO SIGNAL** with a mirror, whistle or even a burning tyre (remove the valve first, though).

Desert creatures like rattlesnakes, scorpions and poisionous spiders should be avoided at all costs. Shake out your boots in the morning and watch your step.

When trekking in the desert prepare for the worst — pack a basic survival kit, and gauge your water needs to the expected daily temperatures.

SURVIVAL IN THE SAHARA

AMERICAN CAPTAIN JAMES RILEY & THE CREW OF THE COMMERCE, WESTERN SAHARA, NORTH AFRICA, 1815

OUTSIDE THE CITY OF MOGADOR, MOROCCO, NOVEMBER 7TH, 1815.

COULD IT REALLY BE THAT THE CREW OF AN *AMERICAN* BRIG HAS CROSSED THE SAHARA?

WILLIAM WILLSHIRE, A BRITISH CONSUL, HAD SOME WEEKS EARLIER RECEIVED A MESSAGE SUPPOSEDLY WRITTEN BY A SHIP'S *CAPTAIN...*

THIS WAY!

HERE ARE THE SAILORS!

GASP!

WITH A SUPREME EFFORT, WILLSHIRE HELD HIS *EMOTIONS* IN CHECK.

"BUT BY MORNING WE FOUND WE WERE NOT ALONE..."

THE NOMADS ARE STRIPPING US OF ALL OUR GEAR. IF ONLY WE HAD **WEAPONS!**

"ATTEMPTING TO CAPTURE ME, THE NOMADS KILLED ONE OF OUR NUMBER, AND THE REST OF US ESCAPED IN THE DAMAGED LONGBOAT."

AAAAAGGGHHHH!

"AFTER DAYS AT SEA, WE FACED A DIFFICULT CHOICE..."

NOTHING, NO PASSING SHIPS AT ALL.

OUR FOOD AND WATER ARE ALMOST GONE, AND THE BOAT IS LEAKING.

WE MUST MAKE FOR THE **SHORE.**

"ON THE NIGHT OF SEPTEMBER 7TH WE APPROACHED THE LAND."

"WE FEARED WE WOULD BE BROKEN UPON THE CRAGGY SHORE, BUT LUCK WAS WITH US."

SWOOOOOSH

"A GREAT SURF ROSE UP AND PUSHED THE BOAT UPON A SMALL FLAT PIECE OF BEACH."

"THE NEXT MORNING WE DIVIDED UP THE LAST OF OUR RATIONS AND SET OFF."

MAYBE TO THE SOUTH WE CAN FIND A PLACE TO DIG FOR WATER.

"ON THE CLIFF TOP A TRACKLESS WASTELAND STRETCHED ENDLESSLY TOWARD THE HORIZON."

THERE'S NOT A LIVING THING IN SIGHT. IT'S TOO MUCH TO BEAR.

"SEVERAL OF MY MEN DROPPED TO THE GROUND AND WEPT, CATCHING THEIR SALTY TEARS, SO THAT THE MOISTURE WAS NOT WASTED."

"WE CONTINUED ALONG THE CLIFF UNTIL NIGHTFALL, WHEN ON A DISTANT BEACH CLARKE SAW..."

LIGHTS, THE LIGHT OF FIRES!

WE WILL APPROACH THE CAMP IN THE MORNING.

"I KNEW WE WOULD BE IN DANGER, BUT I FELT SO **THIRSTY** I COULD HARDLY **BREATHE**."

WATER! WATER!

"I BEGGED."

"TAKING NO NOTICE, THEY BADE US KEEP UP WITH THE CAMELS."

"THE GROUND, WHICH WAS STREWN WITH SHARP STONES, CUT MY FEET LIKE BROKEN GLASS."

"I BROKE DOWN..."

OH, *CURSE* THE FATES. WHY DIDN'T I DROWN AT SEA?

"I SEARCHED FOR A ROCK LARGE ENOUGH TO **BASH** MY OWN BRAINS IN."

"FINDING NONE, I RESTED, AND SOON REASON RETURNED..."

I WILL SUBMIT TO MY *FATE*.

WHATEVER IT MAY BE...

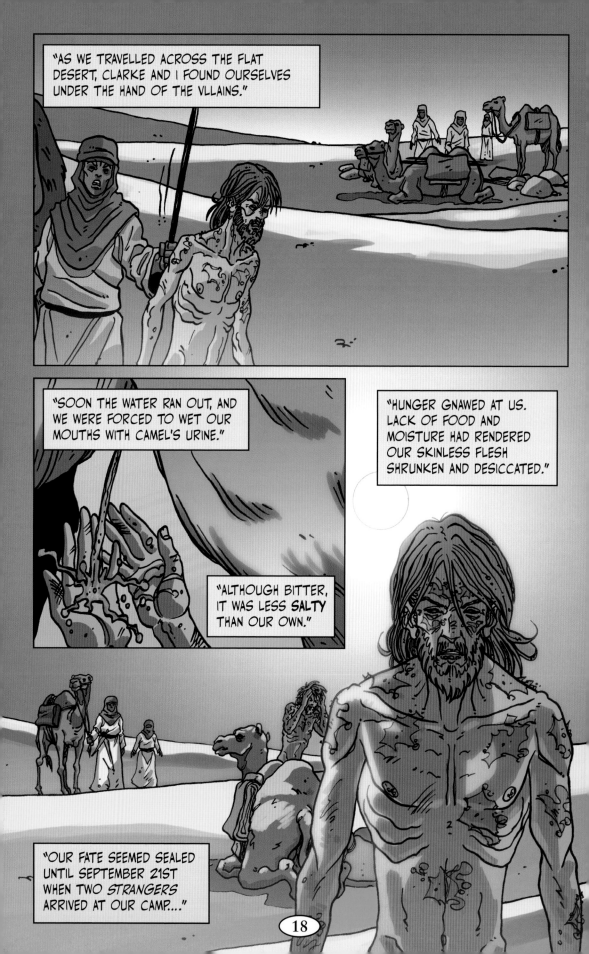

"AS WE TRAVELLED ACROSS THE FLAT DESERT, CLARKE AND I FOUND OURSELVES UNDER THE HAND OF THE VLLAINS."

"SOON THE WATER RAN OUT, AND WE WERE FORCED TO WET OUR MOUTHS WITH CAMEL'S URINE."

"HUNGER GNAWED AT US. LACK OF FOOD AND MOISTURE HAD RENDERED OUR SKINLESS FLESH SHRUNKEN AND DESICCATED."

"ALTHOUGH BITTER, IT WAS LESS **SALTY** THAN OUR OWN."

"OUR FATE SEEMED SEALED UNTIL SEPTEMBER 21ST WHEN TWO **STRANGERS** ARRIVED AT OUR CAMP...."

18

"BY CONCENTRATING ON THEIR WORDS AND ACTIONS, I HAD COME TO UNDERSTAND A LITTLE OF THEIR LANGUAGE."

"THIS WAS HOW I UNDERSTOOD WHEN SIDI HAMET QUESTIONED ME CLOSELY ABOUT HOW I HAD COME TO THIS DESERT."

"HAMET WAS A TRADER FROM THE NORTH WHO WAS TRAVELLING WITH HIS BROTHER, SEID."

"I TOLD HIM ABOUT THE SHIPWRECK AND THE WIFE WHOM I HAD LEFT BEHIND."

IT WAS A SHIP LIKE THIS, WITH **TWO** MASTS...

"I TOLD HIM ABOUT MY FIVE CHILDREN, WHO NOW HAD BEEN LEFT *FATHERLESS*."

"SIDI HAMET SHED A TEAR, AND AN IDEA QUICKLY FORMED IN MY MIND..."

SIDI HAMET, I BEG YOU TO **TAKE** US FROM THIS DESERT.

"THEN IT WAS BOILED..."

EAT, RILEY!

"WORD WENT AROUND THE CAMP."

"SOON THE OTHER ARABS SURROUNDED THE CARCASS."

"THE CAMEL'S STOMACH WAS SLIT OPEN, AND WATER POURED FROM IT TO BOIL THE ENTRAILS IN."

"HAMET BECKONED ME TO THE SLIT..."

DRINK, RILEY!

"THE FRESH BOILED BLOOD, IF ANYTHING, HAD *INCREASED* MY RAGING THIRST. THE LIQUID IN THE CAMEL'S PAUNCH WAS VERY THICK AND STRONG-TASTING, BUT IT WAS NOT BITTER."

"LATER WE EMPTIED THIS WATER INTO GOATSKINS, STRAINING IT THROUGH OUR FINGERS TO KEEP OUT THE WORST OF THE MUCK."

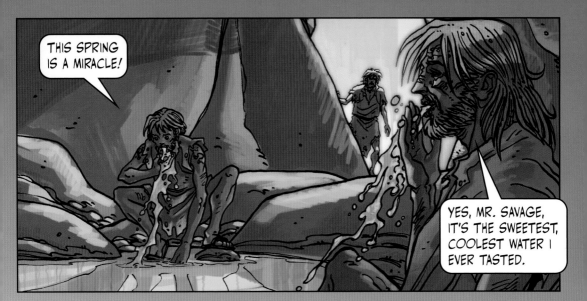

THIS SPRING IS A MIRACLE!

YES, MR. SAVAGE, IT'S THE SWEETEST, COOLEST WATER I EVER TASTED.

"WE VENTURED NORTH, AND ON OCTOBER 4 THE DESERT PRESENTED US WITH A NEW FACE..."

MOUNTAINS ...OF SAND!

"THE TRADE WINDS THAT HAD COOLED US EACH NIGHT NOW WHIPPED THE SAND INTO A TEMPEST."

"THE GRAINS CUT INTO OUR FLESH, PIERCING OUR SORES."

"WE CONTINUED TO CROSS THE SAND HILLS UNTIL OCTOBER 12TH, WHEN WE FINALLY REACHED THE COAST.

"WE HAD MET UP WITH A LARGE CARAVAN OF FRIENDLY NATIVES WHO WERE TRAVELLING TOGETHER FOR SAFETY. WE HAD ENTERED THE DOMAIN OF ROAMING ROBBER BANDS."

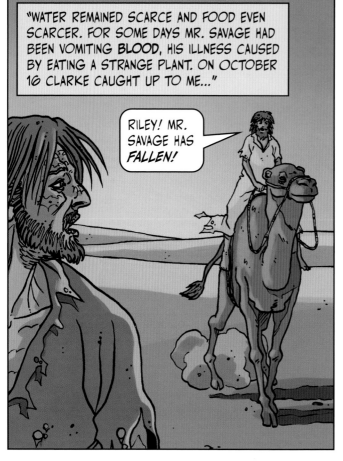

"WATER REMAINED SCARCE AND FOOD EVEN SCARCER. FOR SOME DAYS MR. SAVAGE HAD BEEN VOMITING **BLOOD**, HIS ILLNESS CAUSED BY EATING A STRANGE PLANT. ON OCTOBER 16 CLARKE CAUGHT UP TO ME..."

RILEY! MR. SAVAGE HAS *FALLEN!*

PANT PANT

LOOK — I CAN **RUN!** I WILL RUN AND FETCH THE CAMELS!

LOOK!

GOOD, YOU *SHALL* SEE YOUR WOMAN AND CHILDREN AGAIN.

"AS WE WORKED OUR WAY ALONG THE COAST, THE VISTA OF SAND HILLS SLOWLY CHANGED TO ONE OF DISTANT MOUNTAINS."

"WE HAD SURVIVED THE 1,300-KILOMETRE* JOURNEY. ON OCTOBER 24TH, AT A TOWN NEAR MOGADOR, SIDI HAMET HANDED ME PAPER AND A QUILL."

"I NOW FACED THE MOST DIFFICULT CHALLENGE OF ALL..."

COME, RILEY, YOU MUST WRITE A **LETTER.**

*800-MILE

26

LOST IN THE DESERT

Italian Marathon Runner Mauro Prosperi
Sahara Desert, Morocco, North Africa, April 1994

IT IS THE MORNING OF THE FOURTH DAY OF THE MARATHON DES SABLES, IN THE MOROCCAN SAHARA DESERT, NORTH AFRICA. A 39-YEAR-OLD ITALIAN POLICEMAN, MAURO PROSPERI, IS SEVENTH OUT OF 134 CONTESTANTS, AND HE HAS JUST LEFT THE CHECKPOINT AT THE 32-KM (20-MILE) MARK, CARRYING A LARGE BOTTLE OF WATER.

GOOD JOB, MAURO. YOU'RE CATCHING UP!

YOU'D BETTER CHECK THOSE ROPES. THE WIND'S PICKING UP.

FIFTEEN MINUTES LATER, AND MAURO IS FINDING IT DIFFICULT TO SEE WHERE HE IS GOING.

I CAN HARDLY SEE THE COURSE MARKERS.

THE SANDSTORM BECOMES EVEN STRONGER. MAURO CROUCHES BEHIND A BUSH.

I'LL WAIT HERE UNTIL THE WIND DIES DOWN.

THE SANDSTORM CONTINUES FOR THE NEXT SIX HOURS!

THE RULES SAY TO STAY WHERE YOU ARE UNTIL RESCUED. I HOPE THEY ARRIVE SOON. I'M RUNNING OUT OF WATER.

THE SECOND DAY...

WHUP WHUP WHUP WHUP

HUH? WHAT'S THAT SOUND?

A RESCUE HELICOPTER PASSES NEARBY...

HEY, I'M HERE! I'M HERE!

WHUP

WHUP

BUT THE PILOTS DO NOT SEE HIM.

THE THIRD DAY HE WAKES UP TO SEE BIRDS CIRCLING OVERHEAD...

I'M NOT DEAD YET!

ON THE FOURTH DAY, MAURO SPOTS A PLANE.

HE MAKES AN *SOS* OUT OF ANYTHING HE CAN FIND, BUT THE PILOTS DO NOT SEE THE MESSAGE.

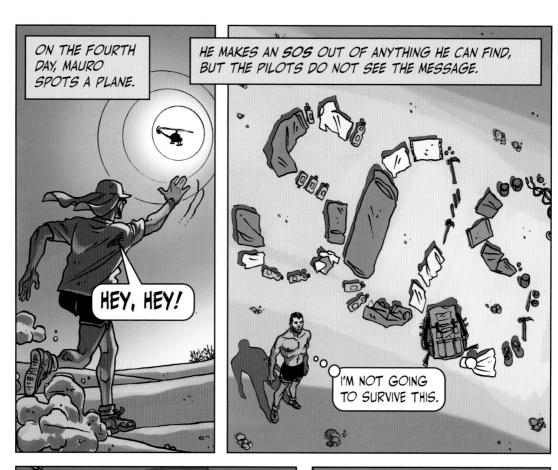

HEY, HEY!

I'M NOT GOING TO SURVIVE THIS.

FOR THE NEXT FOUR DAYS MAURO SURVIVES 46°C (115°F) HEAT AND FREEZING TEMPERATURES AT NIGHT.

I CAN'T BELIEVE I'M S-SO C-C-COLD.

HE COVERS HIMSELF WITH *SAND* TO KEEP WARM AT NIGHT.

IN THE MORNINGS HE LICKS THE DEW FROM PLANTS...

SO THIRSTY...

ONCE OR TWICE HE CATCHES AND KILLS A SNAKE OR A LIZARD...

GOTCHA!

...AND EATS THEM *RAW*.

SNAFFLE

EIGHT DAYS AND 209 KM (130 MILES) AFTER HE BECAME *LOST*, A *NOMADIC* FAMILY FINDS HIM IN A DESPERATE STATE.

WATER?

THEY TAKE HIM TO A VILLAGE. FROM THERE HE IS TAKEN TO A HOSPITAL, WHERE HE SLOWLY *RECOVERS*.

THE END

SURVIVING THE KALAHARI

SOUTH AFRICAN PILOT CARL DU PLESSIS
KALAHARI DESERT, BOTSWANA, AFRICA, MARCH 7TH, 2000

AFTER DEVELOPING ENGINE TROUBLE, A LIGHT AIRCRAFT HAS CRASHED IN A **FOREST CLEARING.**

THE PILOT, BUSINESSMAN CARL DU PLESSIS, HAS ESCAPED. SO HAS HIS COPILOT, COSTA MARCANDONATOS, AND A PASSENGER, MIKE NIKOLIC.

HELP ME! I'M BURNING!

HOWEVER, NIKOLIC'S WIFE, LYNETTE, REMAINS **TRAPPED** IN THE PLANE, ALONG WITH DU PLESSIS'S FRIEND NEB GRAORAC, WHO IS **UNCONSCIOUS.**

THEY WORK TO FREE LYNETTE AND NEB.

ALTHOUGH NOT A **TRUE DESERT**, THE KALAHARI, AS THEY WILL DISCOVER, IS A **VERY BAD** PLACE TO BE **STRANDED**...

NEB'S COMING AROUND!

AAH—MY ARM!

HE CAN'T **BREATHE**, AND THERE'S BLOOD!

HFRRRHHHH!

HE'S HURT HIS CHEST. HELP ME PROP HIM UP!

BANG

CRACKLE

NEB, NEB, IS THAT BETTER?

HE'S NODDING, THANK HEAVENS!

BY BUILDING A FIRE TO SCARE OFF LIONS, THEY GET THROUGH THE NIGHT SAFELY, BUT...

THE DAY'S **HEATING UP.** LYNETTE AND NEB ARE NOT GOING TO LAST LONG OUT HERE WITHOUT WATER.

I'M GOING TO GO AND GET HELP.

I'M GOING TO COME WITH YOU!

COSTA REASONED THAT IF THEY WALKED SOUTHWEST THEY COULD REACH MAUN, THE NEAREST TOWN, IN FOUR DAYS.

GUYS, WE'LL BE BACK AS SOON AS WE FIND HELP. WHATEVER HAPPENS, **KEEP THAT FIRE GOING!**

FOUR HOURS LATER...

CARL, WE'RE NEVER GOING TO GET THROUGH THIS **THICKET.** ARE YOU SURE WE'RE GOING IN THE **RIGHT DIRECTION?**

LOOK, THERE'S AN **ELEPHANT TRACK.** IF WE FOLLOW IT, IT'LL LEAD US TO WATER. I'M **SURE** OF IT.

37

SOON ENOUGH THEY COME UPON A WATER HOLE, BUT...

EUUGH, IT LOOKS DISGUSTING. IT'S **FILTHY DIRTY!**

I DON'T CARE. I'M **DRY AS A BONE.**

ALTHOUGH THE WATER TASTES **VILE** AND IS FULL OF **BACTERIA,** THEY FORCE THEMSELVES TO DRINK IT.

SLURRP

BLUEEEW...

THEY CONTINUE TO FOLLOW THE ELEPHANT TRACK UNTIL...

STOP! DON'T MOVE A MUSCLE.

WRRRRRUUUGH!

A BULL ELEPHANT HAS **SENSED** THEM.

38

QUIETLY, THEY BACK OFF TO WAIT IN THE BUSHES.

THAT NIGHT IT RAINS.

THANK HEAVENS! I MUST FIND SOMETHING TO COLLECT IT IN.

OH, NO, THE FIRE'S GOING OUT. GOT TO KEEP IT LIT!

MIKE MANAGES TO KEEP THE FIRE GOING BUT FAILS TO COLLECT ANY WATER.

THE NEXT DAY IS HOT AND DRY.

NEB HAS HAD TO REMAIN *STANDING* SINCE THE CRASH.

HE HAS NOT SLEPT FOR **THREE DAYS.**

RENDERED DELIRIOUS FROM SLEEP DEPRIVATION AND DEHYDRATION, HE STUMBLES OUT INTO THE BUSH.

HAPPENING UPON A TREE, HE FINDS...

WATER!

HE CALLS THE OTHERS OVER AND THEY DRINK FROM THE SMALL POOL OF WATER.

LYNETTE, YOUR ARM...

HUH!? OH, MY...

OH, BOY...

UGH!

...MAGGOTS!

GET THEM OFF! GET THEM OFF!

ALTHOUGH THEY FRANTICALLY SCRAPE THEM AWAY, THE MAGGOTS WERE ACTUALLY CLEANING THE WOUND OF ROTTED FLESH.

ON THE ELEPHANT TRACK, CARL AND COSTA ARE STILL ONLY 32 KM (20 MILES)* FROM THE CRASH SITE WHEN THEY MEET A FORK IN THE PATH.

SHOULD WE GO LEFT OR RIGHT?

*ALTHOUGH THEY HAVE IN FACT WALKED MORE THAN 96 KM (60 MILES) ON THE ZIGZAG PATH.

THUNKA-
THUNKA-
THUNKA-

BY CHANCE CARL AND COSTA HAD CHOSEN THE **RIGHT** PATH. IT HAD LED THEM TO A REMOTE **HUNTING LODGE**, WHERE THEY HAD RADIOED FOR **HELP**.

WOP-WOP-WOP-

BESIDES HER BURN, LYNETTE ALSO HAD SERIOUS SPINAL INJURIES, AND NEB HAD A PUNCTURED LUNG. OVER TIME, EVERYONE MADE A FULL RECOVERY FOLLOWING THEIR CLOSE ENCOUNTER WITH THE **KALAHARI DESERT**.

THE END

MORE DESERT SURVIVAL STORIES

Compared with jungles and the wilderness, there are relatively few survival stories associated with the desert. The dry, barren emptiness is much more likely to induce panic and hopelessness in those cast unprepared into its wastes. Not to mention the lack of water...

SURVIVING THE GREAT SALT LAKE DESERT, NORTHERN UTAH, AUGUST 1953

American Rodger Jones was driving along a rough desert road when his axle broke. The heat of the day was just beginning. A former Marine who had received basic survival training, Jones got out of his car, lay down in the shadow of the vehicle, and went to sleep. At around 6 p.m. when the sun had waned but the temperature was still around 35°C (95°F), he woke. Walking along the road he came to a steel water tank that had been set up to aid thirsty tourists. He stopped to drink his fill and replenish his water bottle. Jones spent the rest of the long summer evening walking along the road, resting whenever he found shade.

After a while he came upon another water tank, drank, and filled his bottle. As he walked he collected large stones, stopping occasionally to arrange them by the roadside into the word HELP, with an arrow showing his direction of travel. The next day a motorist saw one of these signs and after a four hour drive caught up with Jones, who was quietly resting in the shade of a rock in the 43°C (110°F) heat, none the worse for wear.

HELPLESS IN A GULLY IN MOAB, EASTERN UTAH, DECEMBER 2006

Danelle Ballengee, a 35-year-old American adventure racing champion and longtime resident of Utah, knew the desert well. Setting off from her house one morning for a two-hour run with her dog Taz, Ballengee could not have known that she would spend the next three days fighting desperately for her life.

The weather was frosty. When Ballengee clambered out of a secluded canyon, she stepped on ice and her foot slid out from under her. She slid helplessly down a smooth rock face, tumbled over a ledge, and hit the canyon floor. She didn't know it yet, but she had broken her pelvis. All she knew was that she had to get out of the canyon... and her legs didn't work.

For five hours Ballengee dragged herself through the dirt, until she reached a puddle of melted snow. She drank a little. The temperature was dropping below freezing, and her clothing was thin. She put on a shower cap that she kept in her pack for racing and started doing stomach crunches and rubbing her hands to keep warm. Ballengee's adventure race training enabled her to keep awake and focused like this through the next 52 hours.

On the morning of the third day, weakened by frostbite and her increasingly heavy, painful pelvis, Ballengee seriously began to wonder whether she might actually die. In desperation she yelled at her dog Taz to go get help. Taz promptly vanished and was found hours later wandering by the side of the road by Moab police, who had been alerted to Ballengee's disappearence by a neighbour. The policemen called out to the dog, who ran off back down the trail.

They followed Taz, who led them straight to Ballengee. Airlifted to a Colorado hospital, Ballengee was informed by doctors that she was very lucky. Pelvic injuries like hers were normally fatal if left untreated for more than 10 hours.

STRANDED IN SOUTHERN UTAH, MAY 2008

Retired Pennsylvania couple Ray and Sue Beard had been enjoying the wonders of Grand Staircase-Escalante National Monument area when the GPS they were using led them up a remote, rough track, where they damaged their rental car. They were stranded in the desert.

Panic set in when they realized that no one would be looking for them. For four days and nights they survived in the car on just 24 crackers each and a little Diet Coke. Finally they decided to set off for help, taking five hours to cover 11 km (7 miles) in 32°C (90°F) heat. Luckily they were then rescued by a passing motorcyclist.

GLOSSARY

abound To exist in great numbers.

abrasive Something that roughly rubs or grazes the skin.

barren Not producing any useful vegetation.

brig A two masted, square-rigged sailing ship often used to transport cargo.

carcass The dead body of a slaughtered animal.

chafe To wear and irritate by rubbing.

consul An official appointed by a government to live in a foreign city and protect the government's and its people's interests there.

dehydration Loss of bodily fluids from lack of water.

delirious Badly disturbed mentally and unable to think straight.

desiccated Completely dried out.

domain A ruler's kingdom.

entrails An animal's intestines when taken out of a carcass.

evolved Developed gradually.

festering Rotting, especially an open wound.

gnawed Bit or nibbled at something without stopping.

GPS Global Positioning System. A system of satellites that allows people with specialized receivers to pinpoint exactly where they are on the Earth.

nomads People who have no fixed home and move according to the seasons from place to place in search of food.

paunch The rumen, or first stomach, of an even-toed animal that chews the cud.

ransom A prize, often money, that is demanded or paid for the release of a prisoner.

replenish To fill or add a new supply to.

strewn Scattered here and there without order.

tempest A violent, windy storm.

thicket A dense growth of shrubs or plants.

trekking Making a long, exhausting journey.

ultraviolet Electromagnetic radiation in the sun's rays that can damage bare skin if exposed for too long.

vista A grand scenic view.

FOR MORE INFORMATION

ORGANIZATIONS

Arizona-Sonora Desert Museum
2021 North Kinney Road
Tucson, Arizona 85743
(520) 883-2702
Web site: http://www.desertmuseum.org

National Park Service
1849 C Street NW
Washington, DC 20240
(202) 208-3818
Web site: http://www.nps.gov

FOR FURTHER READING

Gray, Leon, *Deserts* (Geographywise), Wayland, 2010.

Greenberger, Robert, *Deserts, The Living Landscape* (Biomes of the World), Rosen Publishing Company, 2009.

Hinshaw Patent, Dorothy, *Life in a Desert* (Ecosystems in Action Series), Lerner Publications, 2003.

Pipe, Jim, *Daring Journeys* (On the Edge), Evans, 2010.

Serafini, Frank, *Looking Closely Across the Desert*, Kids Can Press Ltd, 2008.

INDEX